Dear Erica

Someday you
will Love these
Poems.

Love
Mommy
Daddy
Christina
Patrice

A CHILD'S GARDEN OF VERSES

ROBERT LOUIS STEVENSON
WITH ILLUSTRATIONS BY
JESSIE WILLCOX SMITH

This edition is distributed by
AVENEL BOOKS
a division of Crown Publishers, Inc.

CONTENTS

BED IN SUMMER

IN winter I get up at night
And dress by yellow candle-light.
In summer, quite the other way,
I have to go to bed by day.

I have to go to bed and see
The birds still hopping on the tree,
Or hear the grown-up people's feet
Still going past me in the street.

And does it not seem hard to you,
When all the sky is clear and blue,
And I should like so much to play,
To have to go to bed by day?

AT THE SEA-SIDE

WHEN I was down beside the sea
A wooden spade they gave to me
To dig the sandy shore.

My holes were empty like a cup.
In every hole the sea came up,
Till it could come no more.

A GOOD PLAY

WE built a ship upon the stairs
    All made of the back-bedroom chairs,
And filled it full of sofa pillows
To go a-sailing on the billows.

We took a saw and several nails,
And water in the nursery pails;
And Tom said, "Let us also take
An apple and a slice of cake;"—
Which was enough for Tom and me
To go a-sailing on, till tea.

We sailed along for days and days
And had the very best of plays;
But Tom fell out and hurt his knee,
So there was no one left but me.

UP into the cherry tree
  Who should climb but little me?
I held the trunk with both my hands
And looked abroad on foreign lands.

I saw the next door garden lie,
Adorned with flowers, before my eye,
And many pleasant places more
That I had never seen before.

I saw the dimpling river pass
And be the sky's blue looking-glass;
The dusty roads go up and down
With people tramping in to town.

If I could find a higher tree
Farther and farther I should see,
To where the grown-up river slips
Into the sea among the ships,

To where the roads on either hand
Lead onward into fairy land,
Where all the children dine at five,
And all the playthings come alive.

SYSTEM

EVERY night my prayers I say,
 And get my dinner every day;
And every day that I've been good,
I get an orange after food.

The child that is not clean and neat,
With lots of toys and things to eat,
He is a naughty child, I'm sure—
Or else his dear papa is poor.

A GOOD BOY

I WOKE before the morning, I was happy all the day,
I never said an ugly word, but smiled and stuck to play.

And now at last the sun is going down behind the wood,
And I am very happy, for I know that I've been good.

My bed is waiting cool and fresh, with linen smooth and fair
And I must be off to sleepsin-by, and not forget my prayer.

I know that, till to-morrow I shall see the sun arise,
No ugly dream shall fright my mind, no ugly sight my eyes.

But slumber hold me tightly till I waken in the dawn,
And hear the thrushes singing in the lilacs round the lawn.

THE LAND OF COUNTERPANE

WHEN I was sick and lay a-bed,
I had two pillows at my head,
And all my toys beside me lay
To keep me happy all the day.

And sometimes for an hour or so
I watched my leaden soldiers go,
With different uniforms and drills,
Among the bed-clothes, through the hills;

And sometimes sent my ships in fleets
All up and down among the sheets;
Or brought my trees and houses out,
And planted cities all about.

I was the giant great and still
That sits upon the pillow-hill,
And sees before him, dale and plain,
The pleasant land of counterpane.

MARCHING SONG

BRING the comb and play upon it!
    Marching, here we come!
Willie cocks his highland bonnet,
    Johnnie beats the drum.

Mary Jane commands the party,
    Peter leads the rear;
Feet in time, alert and hearty,
    Each a Grenadier!

All in the most martial manner
    Marching double-quick;
While the napkin, like a banner,
    Waves upon the stick!

Here's enough of fame and pillage,
    Great commander Jane!
Now that we've been round the village,
    Let's go home again.

HAPPY THOUGHT

THE world is so full of a number of things,
I'm sure we should all be as happy as kings.

JESSIE WILLCOX SMITH.

MY SHADOW

I HAVE a little shadow that goes in and out with me,
And what can be the use of him is more than I can see.
He is very, very like me from the heels up to the head;
And I see him jump before me, when I jump into my bed.

The funniest thing about him is the way he likes to grow—
Not at all like proper children, which is always very slow;
For he sometimes shoots up taller like an india-rubber ball,
And he sometimes gets so little that there's none of him at all.

He hasn't got a notion of how children ought to play,
And can only make a fool of me in every sort of way.
He stays so close beside me, he's a coward you can see;
I'd think shame to stick to nursie as that shadow sticks to me!

One morning, very early, before the sun was up,
I rose and found the shining dew on every buttercup;
But my lazy little shadow, like an arrant sleepy-head,
Had stayed at home behind me and was fast asleep in bed.

THE WIND

I SAW you toss the kites on high
 And blow the birds about the sky;
And all around I heard you pass,
Like ladies' skirts across the grass—
   O wind, a-blowing all day long,
   O wind, that sings so loud a song!

I saw the different things you did,
But always you yourself you hid.
I felt you push, I heard you call,
I could not see yourself at all—
   O wind, a-blowing all day long,
   O wind, that sings so loud a song!

O you that are so strong and cold,
O blower, are you young or old?
Are you a beast of field and tree,
Or just a stronger child than me?
   O wind, a-blowing all day long,
   O wind, that sings so loud a song!

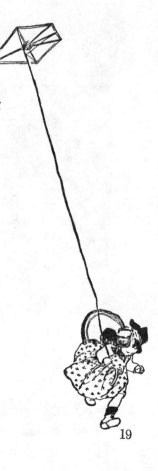

FOREIGN CHILDREN

LITTLE Indian, Sioux or Crow,
  Little frosty Eskimo,
Little Turk or Japanee,
Oh! don't you wish that you were me?

You have seen the scarlet trees
And the lions over seas;
You have eaten ostrich eggs,
And turned the turtles off their legs.

Such a life is very fine,
But it's not so nice as mine:
You must often, as you trod,
Have wearied *not* to be abroad.

You have curious things to eat,
I am fed on proper meat;
You must dwell beyond the foam,
But I am safe and live at home.
   Little Indian, Sioux or Crow,
   Little frosty Eskimo,
   Little Turk or Japanee,
Oh! don't you wish that you were me?

THE MOON

THE moon has a face like the clock in the hall
She shines on thieves on the garden wall,
On streets and field and harbour quays,
And birdies asleep in the forks of the trees.

The squalling cat and the squeaking mouse,
The howling dog by the door of the house,
The bat that lies in bed at noon,
All love to be out by the light of the moon.

But all of the things that belong to the day
Cuddle to sleep to be out of her way;
And flowers and children close their eyes
Till up in the morning the sun shall arise.

TO AUNTIE

CHIEF *of our aunts—not only I,*
    But all your dozen of nurselings cry—
What did the other children do?
And what were childhood, wanting you?

THE UNSEEN PLAYMATE

WHEN children are playing alone on the green,
In comes the playmate that never was seen.
When children are happy and lonely and good,
The Friend of the Children comes out of the wood.

Nobody heard him and nobody saw,
His is a picture you never could draw,
But he's sure to be present, abroad or at home,
When children are happy and playing alone.

He lies in the laurels, he runs on the grass,
He sings when you tinkle the musical glass;
Whene'er you are happy and cannot tell why,
The Friend of the Children is sure to be by!

He loves to be little, he hates to be big,
'Tis he that inhabits the caves that you dig;
'Tis he when you play with your soldiers of tin
That sides with the Frenchmen and never can win.

'Tis he, when at night you go off to your bed,
Bids you go to your sleep and not trouble your head;
For wherever they're lying, in cupboard or shelf,
'Tis he will take care of your playthings himself!

LOOKING-GLASS RIVER

SMOOTH it glides upon its travel,
   Here a wimple, there a gleam—
   O the clean gravel!
   O the smooth stream!

Sailing blossoms, silver fishes,
   Paven pools as clear as air—
   How a child wishes
   To live down there!

We can see our coloured faces
   Floating on the shaken pool
   Down in cool places,
   Dim and very cool;

Till a wind or water wrinkle,
   Dipping marten, plumping trout,
   Spreads in a twinkle
   And blots all out.

See the rings pursue each other;
All below grows black as night,
Just as if mother
Had blown out the light!

Patience, children, just a minute—
See the spreading circles die;
The stream and all in it
Will clear by-and-by.

AUTUMN FIRES

IN the other gardens
    And all up the vale,
From the autumn bonfires
    See the smoke trail!

Pleasant summer over
    And all the summer flowers,
The red fire blazes,
    The grey smoke towers.

Sing a song of seasons!
    Something bright in all!
Flowers in the summer,
    Fires in the fall!

THE HAYLOFT

THROUGH all the pleasant meadow-side
   The grass grew shoulder-high,
Till the shining scythes went far and wide
   And cut it down to dry.

Those green and sweetly smelling crops
   They led in waggons home;
And they piled them here in mountain tops
   For mountaineers to roam.

Here is Mount Clear, Mount Rusty-Nail,
   Mount Eagle and Mount High;—
The mice that in these mountains dwell,
   No happier are than I!

Oh, what a joy to clamber there,
   Oh, what a place for play,
With the sweet, the dim, the dusty air,
   The happy hills of hay!

WINTER-TIME

LATE lies the wintry sun a-bed,
  A frosty, fiery sleepy-head;
Blinks but an hour or two; and then,
A blood-red orange, sets again.

Before the stars have left the skies,
At morning in the dark I rise;
And shivering in my nakedness,
By the cold candle, bathe and dress.

Close by the jolly fire I sit
To warm my frozen bones a bit;
Or with a reindeer-sled, explore
The colder countries round the door.

When to go out, my nurse doth wrap
Me in my comforter and cap;
The cold wind burns my face, and blows
Its frosty pepper up my nose.

Black are my steps on silver sod;
Thick blows my frosty breath abroad;
And tree and house, and hill and lake,
Are frosted like a wedding-cake.

NORTH-WEST PASSAGE

1. Good-night

WHEN the bright lamp is carried in,
The sunless hours again begin;
O'er all without, in field and lane,
The haunted night returns again.

Now we behold the embers flee
About the firelit hearth; and see
Our faces painted as we pass,
Like pictures, on the window-glass.

Must we to bed indeed? Well then,
Let us arise and go like men,
And face with an undaunted tread
The long black passage up to bed.

Farewell, O brother, sister, sire!
O pleasant party round the fire!
The songs you sing, the tales you tell,
Till far to-morrow, fare ye well!

2. *Shadow March*

All round the house is the jet-black night;
   It stares through the window-pane;
It crawls in the corners, hiding from the light,
   And it moves with the moving flame.

Now my little heart goes a-beating like a drum,
   With the breath of the Bogie in my hair;
And all round the candle the crooked shadows come,
   And go marching along up the stair.

The shadow of the balusters, the shadow of the lamp,
  The shadow of the child that goes to bed—
All the wicked shadows coming, tramp, tramp, tramp,
  With the black night overhead.

3. *In Port*

Last, to the chamber where I lie
My fearful footsteps patter nigh,
And come from out the cold and gloom
Into my warm and cheerful room.

There, safe arrived, we turn about
To keep the coming shadows out,
And close the happy door at last
On all the perils that we past.

Then, when mamma goes by to bed,
She shall come in with tip-toe tread,
And see me lying warm and fast
And in the Land of Nod at last.

THE LITTLE LAND

WHEN at home alone I sit,
    And am very tired of it,
I have just to shut my eyes
To go sailing through the skies—
To go sailing far away
To the pleasant Land of Play;
To the fairy land afar
Where the Little People are;
Where the clover-tops are trees,
And the rain-pools are the seas,
And the leaves, like little ships,
Sail about on tiny trips;
And above the daisy tree
    Through the grasses,
High o'erhead the Bumble Bee
    Hums and passes.

In that forest to and fro
I can wander, I can go;
See the spider and the fly,
And the ants go marching by;

Carrying parcels with their feet
Down the green and grassy street.
I can in the sorrel sit
Where the ladybird alit.
I can climb the jointed grass
   And on high
See the greater swallows pass
   In the sky,
And the round sun rolling by
Heeding no such things as I.

Through that forest I can pass
Till, as in a looking-glass,
Humming fly and daisy tree
And my tiny self I see,
Painted very clear and neat
On the rain-pool at my feet.
Should a leaflet come to land
Drifting near to where I stand,
Straight I'll board that tiny boat
Round the rain-pool sea to float.

Little thoughtful creatures sit
On the grassy coasts of it;
Little things with lovely eyes
See me sailing with surprise.
Some are clad in armour green—
(These have sure to battle been!)—
Some are pied with ev'ry hue,
Black and crimson, gold and blue;

Some have wings and swift are gone;—
But they all look kindly on.

When my eyes I once again
   Open, and see all things plain:
High bare walls, great bare floor;
Great big knobs on drawer and door;
Great big people perched on chairs,
Stitching tucks and mending tears,
Each a hill that I could climb,
And talking nonsense all the time—
   O dear me,
   That I could be
A sailor on the rain-pool sea,
A climber in the clover tree,
And just come back, a sleepy-head,
Late at night to go to bed.

MY TREASURES

THESE nuts, that I keep in the back of the nest
Where all my lead soldiers are lying at rest,
Were gathered in autumn by nursie and me
In a wood with a well by the side of the sea.

This whistle we made (and how clearly it sounds!)
By the side of a field at the end of the grounds.
Of a branch of a plane, with a knife of my own,
It was nursie who made it, and nursie alone!

The stone, with the white and the yellow and grey,
We discovered I cannot tell *how* far away;
And I carried it back although weary and cold,
For though father denies it, I'm sure it is gold.

But of all my treasures the last is the king,
For there's very few children possess such a thing;
And that is a chisel, both handle and blade,
Which a man who was really a carpenter made.

PICTURE-BOOKS IN WINTER

SUMMER fading, winter comes—
Frosty mornings, tingling thumbs,
Window robins, winter rooks,
And the picture story-books.

Water now is turned to stone
Nurse and I can walk upon;
Still we find the flowing brooks
In the picture story-books.

All the pretty things put by,
Wait upon the children's eye,
Sheep and shepherds, trees and crooks,
In the picture story-books.

We may see how all things are,
Seas and cities, near and far,
And the flying fairies' looks,
In the picture story-books.

How am I to sing your praise,
Happy chimney-corner days,
Sitting safe in nursery nooks,
Reading picture story-books?

BLOCK CITY

WHAT are you able to build with your blocks?
Castles and palaces, temples and docks.
Rain may keep raining, and others go roam,
But I can be happy and building at home.

Let the sofa be mountains, the carpet be sea,
There I'll establish a city for me:
A kirk and a mill and a palace beside,
And a harbour as well where my vessels may ride.

Great is the palace with pillar and wall,
A sort of a tower on the top of it all,
And steps coming down in an orderly way
To where my toy vessels lie safe in the bay.

This one is sailing and that one is moored:
Hark to the song of the sailors on board!
And see, on the steps of my palace, the kings
Coming and going with presents and things!

Now I have done with it, down let it go!
All in a moment the town is laid low.
Block upon block lying scattered and free,
What is there left of my town by the sea?

Yet as I saw it, I see it again,
The kirk and the palace, the ships and the men,
And as long as I live and where'er I may be,
I'll always remember my town by the sea.

THE LAND OF STORY–BOOKS

AT evening when the lamp is lit,
    Around the fire my parents sit;
They sit at home and talk and sing,
    And do not play at anything.

Now, with my little gun, I crawl
All in the dark along the wall,
And follow round the forest track
Away behind the sofa back.

There, in the night, where none can spy,
All in my hunter's camp I lie,
And play at books that I have read
Till it is time to go to bed.

These are the hills, these are the woods,
These are my starry solitudes;
And there the river by whose brink
The roaring lions come to drink.

I see the others far away
As if in firelit camp they lay,
And I, like to an Indian scout,
Around their party prowled about.

So, when my nurse comes in for me,
Home I return across the sea,
And go to bed with backward looks
At my dear land of Story-books.

THE FLOWERS

ALL the names I know from nurse:
   Gardener's garters, Shepherd's purse,
Bachelor's buttons, Lady's smock,
And the Lady Hollyhock.

Fairy places, fairy things,
Fairy woods where the wild bee wings,
Tiny trees for tiny dames—
These must all be fairy names!

Tiny woods below whose boughs
Shady fairies weave a house;
Tiny tree-tops, rose or thyme,
Where the braver fairies climb!

Fair are grown-up people's trees,
But the fairest woods are these;
Where, if I were not so tall,
I should live for good and all.

NIGHT AND DAY

WHEN the golden day is done,
    Through the closing portal,
Child and garden, flower and sun,
    Vanish all things mortal.

As the blinding shadows fall
    As the rays diminish,
Under evening's cloak, they all
    Roll away and vanish.

Garden darkened, daisy shut,
    Child in bed, they slumber—
Glow-worm in the highway rut,
    Mice among the lumber.

In the darkness houses shine,
    Parents move with candles;
Till on all, the night divine
    Turns the bedroom handles.

Till at last the day begins
     In the east a-breaking,
In the hedges and the whins
     Sleeping birds a-waking.

In the darkness shapes of things,
     Houses, trees and hedges,
Clearer grow; and sparrow's wings
     Beat on window ledges.

These shall wake the yawning maid;
     She the door shall open—
Finding dew on garden glade
     And the morning broken.

There my garden grows again
     Green and rosy painted,
As at eve behind the pane
     From my eyes it fainted.

Just as it was shut away,
     Toy-like, in the even,
Here I see it glow with day
     Under glowing heaven.

Every path and every plot,
     Every bush of roses,
Every blue forget-me-not
     Where the dew reposes.

"Up!" they cry, "the day is come
  On the smiling valleys:
We have beat the morning drum;
  Playmate, join your allies!"

THE SWING

HOW do you like to go up in a swing,
  Up in the air so blue?
Oh, I do think it the pleasantest thing
  Ever a child can do!

Up in the air and over the wall,
  Till I can see so wide,
Rivers and trees and cattle and all
  Over the countryside—

Till I look down on the garden green,
  Down on the roof so brown—
Up in the air I go flying again,
  Up in the air and down!

TIME TO RISE

A BIRDIE with a yellow bill
Hopped upon the window sill,
Cocked his shining eye and said:
"Ain't you 'shamed, you sleepy-head!"

MY KINGDOM

DOWN by a shining water well
   I found a very little dell,
 No higher than my head.
The heather and the gorse about
In summer bloom were coming out,
 Some yellow and some red.

I called the little pool a sea;
The little hills were big to me;
 For I am very small.

I made a boat, I made a town,
I searched the caverns up and down,
   And named them one and all.

And all about was mine, I said,
The little sparrows overhead,
   The little minnows too.
This was the world and I was king;
For me the bees came by to sing,
   For me the swallows flew.

I played there were no deeper seas,
Nor any wider plains than these,
   Nor other kings than me.
At last I heard my mother call
Out from the house at evenfall,
   To call me home to tea.

And I must rise and leave my dell,
And leave my dimpled water well,
   And leave my heather blooms.
Alas! and as my home I neared,
How very big my nurse appeared.
   How great and cool the rooms!

TO ANY READER

AS from the house your mother sees
    You playing round the garden trees,
So you may see, if you will look
Through the windows of this book,
Another child, far, far away,
And in another garden, play.
But do not think you can at all,
By knocking on the window, call
That child to hear you. He intent
Is all on his play-business bent.
He does not hear; he will not look,
Nor yet be lured out of his book.
For, long ago, the truth to say,
He has grown up and gone away,
And it is but a child of air
That lingers in the garden there.